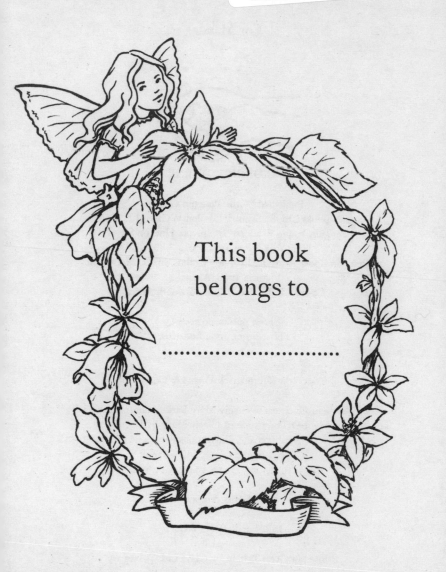

This book
belongs to

....

For Manda

FREDERICK WARNE

Published by the Penguin Group
Penguin Books Ltd, 80 Strand, London WC2R 0RL, England
Penguin Young Readers Group, 345 Hudson Street,
New York, New York 10014, U.S.A.
Penguin Books Australia Ltd, 707 Collins Street, Melbourne,
Victoria 3008, Australia
Canada, India, New Zealand, South Africa

First published 2007
This edition published 2014
001

ISBN: 978 07232 9834 2

Printed in Great Britain by Clays Ltd, St Ives plc

Almond Blossom's Mystery

by Kay Woodward

Welcome to the Flower Fairy Garden!

Where are the fairies?
Where can we find them?
We've seen the fairy-rings
They leave behind them!

Is it a secret
No one is telling?
Why, in your garden
Surely they're dwelling!

No need for journeying,
Seeking afar:
Where there are flowers,
There fairies are!

Contents

Chapter One

The Longest Winter   1

Chapter Two

A Grand Plan   15

Chapter Three

The Outside World   27

Chapter Four

A Big Adventure   39

Chapter Five

Caught   53

Chapter Six

Back to the Garden   65

Chapter One
The Longest Winter

None of the Flower Fairies could remember winter being this long. The bitterly cold weather seemed to have gone on for an eternity. It was months since they'd opened their presents beneath the decorated boughs of the Christmas tree, while the rusty colours of autumn were just a distant memory. It wouldn't have been so bad if the sun was shining, but that was missing too, hidden behind a thick layer of dull cloud.

At first the Flower Fairies, who are usually very optimistic creatures, were hopeful that spring was just around the corner. Then, when the cold, dreary weather continued, they became puzzled. Finally, they began to worry. Would it be winter forever? Without

the sun, how would their garden flourish?
Would the buds and blossoms never appear?
The fairies whispered in hushed voices
to each other, each desperate to learn the
answer to the most important question of all:
where was spring?

There was one Flower Fairy in particular
who was very concerned about the long
winter. And that was Almond Blossom. Day
after day, she peered up at the grim, grey
sky and then looked closely at the bare
branches of her tree.

'Nothing,' she sighed. 'Not even
a bud.' The pretty little fairy, no
bigger than a human hand,
slumped despondently
against the tree trunk.

Spring was the most
important event on
Almond Blossom's

calendar. Every
year, as soon as
winter waved
farewell, the milder
weather encouraged
her delicate, pink
blossoms to unfurl. For all the
other Flower Fairies, this was the very
first sign of spring. For Almond Blossom,
it was her signal to perform the traditional
dance that heralded the new season. She so
enjoyed skipping and pirouetting around
the garden, brandishing one of her own
blossom-laden stems to the sound of the
delighted cheers of the other fairies. It just
wouldn't be the same carrying a bare, brown
twig.

'Cheer up!' called Sycamore from his
lofty perch on a nearby tree. 'It might never
happen!'

'That's what I'm worried about . . .' Almond Blossom replied. 'What if spring never happens – ever? What then?' Her pretty face crumpled and she sobbed great, fat tears of sorrow. 'What'll I do? I may as well just pack up my things and leave the Flower Fairies' Garden!'

Sycamore looked utterly horrified at the effect his seemingly harmless greeting had had on poor Almond Blossom, and he leapt the short distance between their trees, his gauzy wings glowing gold and green in the pale light. 'There, there,' he said, patting her shoulder awkwardly. Sycamore was at

his happiest when fluttering and twirling
through the air, a little like the winged seeds
that whirled from his tree every autumn –
he didn't have much experience in making
glum fairies laugh. But he did
his best.

'Spring will come,' he
said gently. 'Just you
wait and see.'

'That's very kind of
you, Sycamore,' said
Almond Blossom,

wiping away her tears. She grabbed a dark
green leaf and blew her nose into it noisily.
'I don't know what's got into me ... I think
perhaps that I might be missing the sun!'
She laughed weakly.

Sycamore gave her an encouraging grin.
'Soon, it'll be so sunny that you'll wish for a
cloud to come by, to give you some shade!'
he said.

But the dull, cloudy, cold weather
continued. The only variation from the
greyness was the odd, sharp shower that
soaked and chilled any Flower Fairy unlucky
enough to be out in the open.

Almond
Blossom tried
to keep her
spirits up by
practising
the steps of
her spring
dance, but her
heart wasn't
in it. Bleakly,
she noticed that
her fairy outfit was
beginning to look very
shabby. The pale pink petals of
her tutu looked crumpled rather than frothy,
while the petals adorning her chestnut
locks were damp and bedraggled because
of the rain. As for her dusky pink tunic, it
had most definitely seen better days. Tansy
– who was a whiz with needle and thread

– offered to repair her clothes with some of Snowdrop's snowy-white petals, but Almond Blossom politely refused. It wouldn't feel right wearing someone else's petals. No, she would make herself a brand-new outfit when her own blossoms bloomed. Just as she did every year.

Then the crisis deepened. One murky morning, when the weather was so dark and gloomy that the Flower Fairies had to use pinches of precious fairy dust to light their way, word spread around the garden that an emergency meeting was to take place at the blackthorn bush.

As soon as she heard the news, Almond
Blossom hopped down to the ground,
smoothed down her ragged clothes and –
peeping in a puddle on the way to make sure
that she didn't look too scruffy – scurried
towards the blackthorn bush. By the time she
arrived, a large crowd of Flower Fairies had
gathered. They muttered to each other in low
voices.

'What's going on?' Almond Blossom asked Windflower, an elegant fairy with long dark hair and mahogany, patterned wings.

Windflower shrugged. 'I heard there was going to be some big announcement,' she said. 'But I haven't a clue what it's about.'

'Shhhh!' whispered Blackthorn. She sat on a low branch, almost hidden by the tiny white and pink flowers that smothered her plant – one of the very few to bear flowers at this chilly time of year. 'Someone's coming!'

'Greetings!' A powerful voice rang out, silencing the waiting crowd immediately. Heads swivelled round to see who had spoken and then there was a collective gasp. A dazzling Flower Fairy stood before them. He was clothed in shimmering gold and wore a crown of yellow flower stamens on his golden hair. It was Kingcup – the king of the Flower Fairies! 'Please be seated,' the royal visitor continued.

Obediently, everyone sat.

Almond Blossom's throat was as dry as
sandpaper and she swallowed with difficulty.
It didn't take a fairy diploma to know that
bad news was coming.

'Flower Fairies, we have a problem,' said
Kingcup, his kind eyes clouded with concern.
'I'm sure you've noticed that winter has gone
on for a very long time. For some weeks, I
was convinced that it was just an odd weather
pattern and that any day we'd see dear

Almond Blossom dancing merrily through the garden, followed swiftly by glorious spring weather.' He paused to smile briefly at her. 'But now I know different. Prepare yourselves, Flower Fairies, for the truth is shocking.'

Everyone held their breath.

'Spring isn't late,' said Kingcup. 'Spring has been stolen!'

Chapter Two
A Grand Plan

There was a stunned silence as the fairies absorbed the awful news. This wasn't the sort of thing that happened in the Flower Fairies' Garden.

'I'm afraid there's more,' said Kingcup apologetically. 'Unfortunately, this year's Spring Party will have to be postponed until spring is restored to its rightful place, at least. I'm most terribly sorry.'

There was a strangled sob in the middle of the crowd as one Flower Fairy was overwhelmed by the bad tidings.

Shakily, Almond Blossom reached an arm into the air. 'If you please, sir,' she began.

Kingcup looked in her direction and nodded.

'It's just that ... er ... what I-I-I'd like to know ... that is, what I'm sure everyone w-would like to know is ...' Almond Blossom paused, wishing that she felt braver. 'How do you know? Why was spring stolen? Who did it? When? And where –'

'Whoa!' said Kingcup, his handsome face creasing into a brief smile. 'Let me try to answer those questions before you think of any more.' He reached into a pocket and pulled out a scroll of parchment tied with a long ribbon of grass. Slowly, thoughtfully, he held the parchment aloft. 'This,' he said, 'is a ransom note. It explains everything – I think it's best if I read it aloud.'

There were nods of approval from the crowd.

Dear Flower Fairies

My, what a long, cold winter! And do you know why? It's because we've stolen spring and hidden it from you. Ha ha! You'll never find it. But we're prepared to do a deal. In exchange for spring, we want six sacks filled to the brim - no cheating! - with fairy dust.

On Saturday evening at sunset, you must leave these sacks beneath the almond blossom tree. By Sunday morning, spring will return. No fairy dust means no spring.

Do not try to find us, or we will steal summer too.

Signed

As if we'd tell you!

Kingcup rolled up the parchment and tucked it back into his pocket. 'So, dear Flower Fairies,' he said, 'we have these dastardly thieves to thank for our worst-ever winter. And now we need to work out what to do.'

'Why that's simple!' piped up Rose, a friendly little fairy who loved to make others happy. 'If everyone works extra-hard, we should just about have enough fairy dust by Saturday. I have some large leaves that we could make into sturdy sacks. And perhaps the blackbirds would help carry the sacks from flower to flower, until they are full.'

'No way!' Sycamore cried indignantly. He leapt to his feet and looked stern. 'We can't give in to their demands! We must send out a search party immediately and hunt high and low until we've tracked down the thieves.'

'But then they'll steal summer!' wailed Daisy.

'I-I-I'm not sure I can make s-six sacks of f-fairy dust in a w-w-week . . .' White Clover's round, rosy cheeks were awash with tears.

'We want to go to the Spring Party!' sobbed the Sweet Pea babies.

It was pandemonium. Everywhere Almond Blossom looked, there were Flower Fairies shouting or crying into their petal handkerchiefs. She looked round for Kingcup and saw that he was refereeing a squabble between Yew Fairy and Pine Tree Fairy. She scratched her head thoughtfully. If they were to rescue spring and save the party, somebody needed to do something right now . . .

'Please be quiet!' bellowed Almond Blossom at the top of her voice. And everyone was so astonished by the mild-mannered fairy's command that they stopped shouting and arguing and crying immediately. 'Thank you,' she continued meekly. 'I have a plan, if anyone would like to hear it?'

At once, a sea of heads nodded.

'Gather round,' whispered Almond Blossom. 'We don't want to be overheard ...'

By noon, it was settled. Most of the Flower Fairies would set to work making heaps of sparkling fairy dust. They decided it was best if they obeyed the ransom letter's demands – or at least pretended to. Any enemy spies that might be lurking would be fooled into thinking that the fairies had given in, while meanwhile Almond Blossom would search for spring!

'Aren't you even a tiny bit nervous?' asked Windflower, watching as Almond Blossom packed a small bag

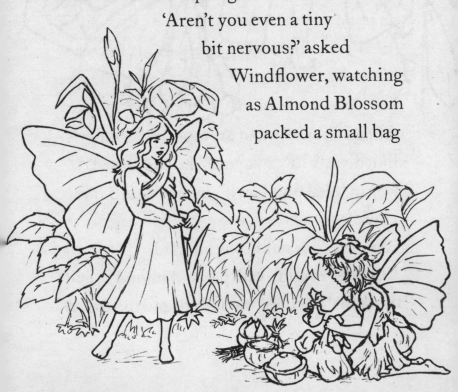

with fairy cheese,
hazelnuts and a nutcase
filled with Elderberry's sweet
juice.

Almond Blossom checked all around
before nodding. 'Oh yes!' she said. 'But I'm
excited too.' It was true. She'd never done
anything like this before – never been on a
secret mission, never been trusted with such
an important task. She could hardly wait!

'What will you do?' asked Windflower.
'Where will you go?' Of all the other Flower
Fairies, she was perhaps the most eager for
Almond Blossom to succeed, for her star-
like, white flowers appeared when the first
breeze of spring blew.

'First, I'm going to search the Flower
Fairies' Garden thoroughly,' replied Almond
Blossom, 'just to make sure the thieves left
no clues. Then I'll travel further afield – and

I won't stop until I've found spring.' She smiled at Windflower as she shouldered her bag. 'Don't worry – the blackbirds are going to fly above me. If I need help, I'll whistle for them.'

'Take this,' Windflower said hastily, thrusting a small, silky-soft bag into her friend's hand. 'It's fairy dust. It's not much, I'm afraid, but it's all I have.

Go on, run – and take care!' She leapt from
the bare branch and somersaulted through
the air, landing neatly on the ground below.
'Farewell!' she cried, before hurrying away.

Almond Blossom smiled as she looked at
Windflower's gift. Everybody was being so
kind – she just hoped that she could repay
them by returning with spring!

Chapter Three
The Outside World

By the time Almond Blossom had explored the Flower Fairies' Garden, not a leaf or a stone or a fallen petal was left unturned. But she didn't find a single clue. Whoever had stolen spring had done a very good job of covering their tracks.

It's time to go over the wall, thought Almond Blossom to herself, trudging towards the far side of the garden. Here, the wall backed on to open marshes, where only the occasional winding lane interrupted the wild countryside. Flower Fairies lived here too – among the reeds and wild grasses, and nestling under flowers of the hedgerow and wayside. Many of these fairies visited the garden from time to time. Secretly, Almond

Blossom hoped to bump into them on her travels – it would be lovely to see a friendly face or two.

She gazed up at the ancient wall, relieved to see that there were plenty of hollows to slip her fingers and toes inside. Briskly, she climbed up the rough stones, stopping only when she reached the top.

'Phew!' said Almond Blossom, perching on the wall to admire the view. Far below her dangling feet was a wide, muddy track, its surface furrowed and uneven. Through the light mist that hung before her, she could make out a dark green hedgerow opposite. It was interwoven with bindweed – white, cushiony blooms that were bold enough and pushy enough to grow absolutely anywhere. She was wondering if White Bindweed Fairy was at home when a wisp of white mist engulfed her. Brrrr! She shivered at its cold touch. It seemed as if the rest of Flower Fairyland was in winter's steely grip too. Almond Blossom couldn't help feeling a little disappointed – she'd hoped that there might be a smidgen of warmth on the other side of the wall.

Ding ding! Ding-a-ling! Ding!

Abruptly, the silence of the quiet

countryside was
shattered by a
frantic jangling of
bells.

'Hurry up, Mark!'
The anxious voice echoed along the track,
accompanied by more ding-a-ling-ing.
'We'll be late!'

'I'm coming!' replied another voice.

Humans! She'd never seen or heard one
before, but others had told her how big
and noisy they were. And, according to
Flower Fairy Law, she must stay out of
sight. If humans knew that fairies really did
exist, their fragile world might be crushed
underfoot by stampeding feet or harmed by
curious fingers.

With nowhere to hide and no time to flee,
Almond Blossom had no other choice but to
fold her wings shut and curl herself into the

tightest possible ball. And then she waited.

The ground began to tremble horribly and there was an ear-splitting screech. 'I really need new brakes,' muttered a voice. The Flower Fairy couldn't resist peeking and saw a girl with dark, silky hair and big blue eyes. She was crouching over a bright blue contraption that Almond Blossom knew must be a bicycle. The girl's face broke into a wide grin as a younger boy skidded to a halt beside her. They looked so alike that they had to be brother and sister. 'Where's Toby?' she asked.

'Not far away,' replied the boy. 'He was barking at some mushrooms a little way back. 'Oh, here he comes!'

A caramel-coloured dog with floppy ears bounded out of the mist, sitting – splat! – in a puddle beside the children. He panted breathlessly, his tongue lolling to one side.

I don't know what all the fuss is about, Almond Blossom thought to herself. *Humans seem perfectly harmless. Pleasant, even. And I rather like their d–*

'Woof! Woof-woof!'
Toby the dog had
begun to make
the most awful
racket that
she'd ever

heard. 'Ow-ow-ow-WOOOOO!' he howled.

Almond Blossom's heart sank as, too late, she remembered how finely tuned animals' senses were. Now the dog was staring right at Almond Blossom. He'd seen her!

'What is it, Toby?' asked the boy. 'You silly dog! There aren't any mushrooms up there ... or are there?' He stood on tiptoes and squinted at the top of the wall.

Any second now, they would start clambering towards her and then they would find her and before nightfall she would be on display in a museum – Almond Blossom just knew it! Unless ... Quickly, she delved her hand deep into the silken bag that

Windflower had given her. She scooped a handful of precious fairy dust into her palm and blew with all her might.

Whoosh!

A cloud of tiny pollen fragments billowed outwards.

'Fairy dust, fairy dust, hide me from sight!' Almond Blossom whispered. At once, the air all around her began to glimmer and shimmer magically.

'What are you looking at, Mark?' asked the girl curiously.

'Er ... nothing,' replied her brother.

'I could have sworn that I saw something . . .'
He paused and frowned, scratching his head.
'Something really strange. But now it's gone
– I must have been mistaken.'

Toby the dog had stopped barking now

and was happily snuffling the ground at the
children's feet.

Almond Blossom smiled to herself.
'Thank you, Windflower,' she whispered
in the tiniest of voices. The fairy dust had
worked its magic brilliantly – she was totally
shielded from view.

'Come on, then,' said the girl. 'Let's escape
this murky weather – I want to see the sun
again.' She leapt back on to her bicycle.
'Race you?'

As the children and their dog vanished round the corner, Almond Blossom rubbed her chin thoughtfully. Something was bothering her, but she couldn't for the life of her work out what it was . . .

Chapter Four
A Big Adventure

Almond Blossom peered into the darkening gloom. This was not good. Night was falling and she hadn't even reached the marsh yet. And, with only two days to go before Saturday's deadline, she didn't have a moment to lose. She grasped a piece of ivy that clung to the stone wall and expertly abseiled down its length, landing with a tiny splish on the sodden ground below. Shouldering her bag once more, she skipped and fluttered across the track to the safety of the hedgerow.

'Yoohoo!' shouted White Bindweed, who was busy weaving flowers in and out of the hedge. 'Are you staying for tea?'

'That's very kind of you,' replied Almond Blossom, 'but I can't stop. I'm searching for spring.'

'Oh, I see,' said White Bindweed, screwing up her face as if she didn't really see at all. She shrugged and grinned. 'OK, then. Catch you later!'

Almond Blossom fought her way through the hedge, which for someone as small as a Flower Fairy was more like a huge and very spooky forbidden forest. Sturdy branches blocked her path, while twigs sprang at her and tore her already tattered clothes. And it was so dark. Bravely, she pushed on, reminding herself that the happiness of the Flower Fairies and the magnificent Spring Party were at stake. She had to succeed.

At last, she reached the other side of the hedge. The overcast sky was charcoal grey now – soon it would be black – but there was just enough light for Almond Blossom to see a little way. She plonked herself down on a handy rock and admired the view. So this was the fabled marsh. A carpet of moss stretched away from her, dotted with clumps of tall grass. Large, lumpy shapes loomed in the distance. For a moment, she feared they might be giants or ogres or some other scary creatures, but then realized that they were probably just trees. She giggled to herself, as excitement fizzed through her once more. This was a grand adventure, all right.

'Time to go!' she announced to the empty wilderness. She leapt to her feet and marched away from the hedge, trying hard not to lose her balance on the springy moss.

Almond Blossom soon learned that unlike the Flower Fairies' Garden, which was quite flat, the marsh was a totally different story. Hollows nestled between grassy hillocks, some of which were mountainous. She struggled to the top of the highest of these mounds, deciding that it would be a perfect spot to camp for the night. But when she reached the top, all thoughts of sleep instantly vanished from her mind.

'What is it?' breathed the little Flower Fairy. A bright stripe of sparkling colour split the darkness, stretching from left to right across the distant horizon. Almond Blossom had never seen anything so

wonderful. It glittered like the brightest
jewel and burned as bright as the biggest
candle. It was vivid pink and luscious orange
and deepest mauve.

It was beautiful.

But she still didn't know what it was.
Dazzled and bewildered, Almond Blossom
sank on to the comfortable moss and stared.
Little by little, the mysterious glow faded
from view, the colours darkening, the light
dimming ... until it was gone. Then, tired

beyond belief, she
slept.

'Wakey, wakey, rise and
shine!' sang a friendly voice.

'Hmmn?' groaned Almond Blossom.
She looked up groggily to see two of the
scruffiest Flower Fairies she'd ever laid eyes
on staring down at her. 'Who are you?' she
asked.

'I'm Rush-Grass,' announced the dark-
haired fairy. He reached down to shake
Almond Blossom's hand, pumping it up and
down enthusiastically. 'Pleased to meet you.'

'And I'm Cotton-Grass,' said the other

fairy, with a cheeky grin. His hair was ash-blond and stood up from his head as if he'd had a very big fright. 'We're brothers.'

Almond Blossom smiled back, noticing

absent-mindedly that the two Flower Fairies had very pointy ears. And although their wings were quite plain, their clothes blended in perfectly with the colours of the marsh grasses – chestnut brown, moss green and deep maroon. In fact, they seemed so at home on the marsh, that she knew without asking that they must be locals.

'You're not from round here, are you?' said Rush-Grass, reminding her that she hadn't introduced herself yet.

'Oh, I'm sorry,' she said. 'How very rude of me. I'm Almond Blossom – I come from the Flower Fairies' Garden.' She sprang to her feet and curtseyed politely.

'There's no need for that,' said Cotton-Grass, with a stifled giggle. 'You're on the marsh now – we're much more laid-back here than the fairies in your garden.' He gave his brother a sideways glance. 'Are you going to ask her?'

Rush-Grass nodded. 'What are you doing here?' he asked curiously. 'Are you lost? Because if you're lost, we'd be delighted to lead you to safety. That's our job, you see.'

Almond Blossom shook her head.

'And if you're not lost,' added Cotton-Grass, 'then we're pretty good guides too. We can show you all the sights – the twisty marsh path, the fairy rings, the elves' secret hideaway, Mallow's famous fairy cheese –'

'What?' Almond Blossom spluttered. Of course! How could she have been so forgetful?

'It's delicious,' said Cotton-Grass, rubbing his tummy and making mmmmm noises. 'Mallow's seeds make the most excellent cheese – the best in Flower Fairyland –'

'No, not the cheese,' interrupted Almond Blossom again. 'The elves! Can you help me to find them?'

'But of course,' replied Rush-Grass. He gave an exasperated sigh and rolled his eyes. 'What have they done now?' he asked.

'Well, they may have done nothing,' began Almond Blossom uncertainly. She was a very fair fairy and liked to give everyone a chance, but the elves were well known throughout the Flower Fairies' Garden for their tricks and monkey business.

This was just the sort of mischief they loved. 'I have a feeling that they might be able to point me in the right direction,' she added.

Noticing that the brothers were looking quite confused,

Almond Blossom told them how the Flower Fairies had received a ransom note and how there were no clues in their garden and how she'd ventured over the wall and on to the marsh to search for any sign of spring or the wicked thieves who'd stolen it. 'Surely you must have noticed how long winter has lasted?' she said.

'Oh, yes,' said Cotton-Grass. 'The weather's dreadful here, isn't it?' He looked up at the thick grey clouds above them. 'It's much nicer on the other side of the marsh. We should take you there.' He pointed. 'Look!'

Almond Blossom looked. She blinked. Then she looked again. There, in the distance, was a sunny strip of yellow, just visible at the edge of the low, grey cloud. Was it . . . ? Could it really be . . . ? It was!

'Hurray!' she cheered, fluttering into the

air with joy. 'It's springtime! We've found spring!'

Chapter Five
Caught

At once, everything slotted into place . . .
Spring hadn't been stolen – it was simply
hidden behind a thick blanket of grey cloud.
This explained why the children had hurried
to escape the murky weather and find the
sun. It also explained why it seemed as if
winter had lasted so long this year.

'The beautiful stripe of colour was the
sunset . . .' breathed Almond Blossom. It
was such an age since she'd
seen the evening sun, she'd
forgotten how magnificent it
could be. She was so pleased
that she couldn't resist a
happy skip and a hop,
much to the delight of

her new fairy friends.

Then she sat down and thought. And thought. But no matter how she puzzled and pondered, mused and mulled it over, she kept coming back to the same conclusion. Whoever had sent the ransom note to the Flower Fairies must also have hung the great dark cloud above their garden.

'Will you help me to find the thieves?' she asked the marsh fairies. 'I want to ask the elves what they know, but I don't know where to find them.'

Rush-Grass and Cotton-Grass nodded solemnly.

'We'll take you there as soon as you've had breakfast,' said Rush-Grass sensibly. 'It's really not a good idea to do this sort of thing on an empty stomach.'

So, as soon as Almond Blossom had nibbled a hazelnut and sipped the cool spring

water that Cotton-Grass brought her, they set off across the marsh. They trekked past tall waving grasses and around squidgy bogs, the two brothers making sure that she didn't stray away from the path and into danger.

It didn't take long to reach the edge of
the cloud, where the marsh was bathed in
glorious sunshine. Almond Blossom paused
for a moment, closing her eyes and raising
her face up to the gentle warmth of the sun.

'There,' Cotton-Grass whispered.

Almond Blossom blinked a little as her
eyes got used to the brightness. 'Where?'
she whispered back, scanning the area all
around them.

Cotton-Grass pointed to an innocent-
looking cluster of toadstools a short

distance away.

They were quite the prettiest things Almond Blossom had seen all morning, with their chocolatey-brown stems and their cherry-red caps, dotted all over with large white spots. The colours dazzled in the spring sunshine.

'Quite poisonous, of course,' muttered Rush-Grass. 'And the perfect place for those naughty elves to hide their secret headquarters.'

'We don't know they've done anything wrong,' said Almond Blossom.

'Hmmm.' Cotton-Grass didn't sound so sure. 'Then let's go and find out,' he said, marching towards the toadstools.

But before they even reached the elves' secret hideaway,

gleeful voices rang out loud and clear.

'We've fooled them!'

'Tomorrow we'll have six sacks of fairy dust!'

'We are so clever! Ha ha haaa!'

Almond Blossom crept closer and peered between the toadstools. And there, in a small clearing, were three green-clad creatures with pointy ears and pointy wings. They were laughing fit to burst. 'You're not that clever,' she said sweetly.

The elves spun round. 'Oh,' said the tallest of the three.

'Oh, indeed,' said Almond Blossom, squeezing through a narrow gap into the hideaway. She put her hands on her hips and frowned at the guilty-looking trio. 'Why did you do it?' she asked.

'We only wanted some fairy dust,' mumbled the shortest elf, staring down at

his feet. 'It's not fair, you know,' he said. 'You
Flower Fairies have all the fun, with your

singing and dancing in your wonderful
garden.'

He looked up and glared at Almond
Blossom, who was suddenly feeling a little
sorry for the miserable creatures.

'We thought it would be funny if we were

enjoying the lovely spring weather, while you were stuck under a wintry cloud,' he continued. 'And it was funny. We haven't been able to stop laughing.' He looked at his two side-kicks. 'Have we, lads?'

'Er, yes...' said the tall elf quickly. 'I mean, no, boss.'

'Ho ho ho,' the third elf laughed unconvincingly. 'Hee hee.'

'But why did you write the ransom note?' asked Almond Blossom, curious now. 'Why didn't you just hide the sun and be done with it? Why did you want the fairy dust too? Elves have their own magic dust, don't they?'

'It's not as sparkly as

yours,' grumbled the chief elf. 'And it's not quite as magical either. Besides, we've only got about a thimbleful left – it took heaps of elf dust to cast the Winter Cloud Spell.' He paused and looked suddenly cunning. 'Why don't you tell us how to make fairy dust . . . ? Because if we knew how to make it, we wouldn't need yours, would we?'

'Nice try!' Almond Blossom laughed. 'But I'm afraid that only Flower Fairies can make fairy dust – and how we make it is a closely guarded secret.'

'Hmmmph,' said the elf.

Almond Blossom thought deeply. Here was a problem indeed. How was she to convince the elves to lift the cloud that covered the Flower Fairies' Garden without collecting the six sacks of fairy dust they'd demanded? Unless...

Almond Blossom reached into her bag and pulled out the silky bag that Windflower had given her.

'Listen very carefully,' she said mysteriously. 'I have an idea...'

Chapter Six
Back to the Garden

Almond Blossom ran her fingertips over her velvet-soft tunic and gently touched the tiny petals sewn around the neck. Then she whirled around, grinning with delight as the pink petals of her skirt spun outwards. Her new outfit was perfect.

She was ready.

Carefully breaking off a twig from her tree – she made sure to choose one that was heavily laden with brand-new blossom –

Almond Blossom
clutched it tightly
before leaping into the air.
Gracefully, she fluttered
downwards, landing lightly
far below, where green shoots were
beginning to poke through the soil.
Almond Blossom raised herself on
tiptoes, took a deep breath and began to
sing the words that the Flower Fairies had
waited so long to hear:

'Joy! the Winter's nearly gone!
Soon will Spring come dancing on;
And, before her, here dance I,
Pink like sunrise in the sky.
Other lovely things will follow;
Soon will cuckoo come, and swallow;
Birds will sing and buds will burst,
But the Almond is the first!'

Happily, she danced through the garden, twirling and high-stepping as she went, hopping and leaping, spinning and swaying.

'Almond Blossom!' cried Sycamore as she jigged past. 'Am I glad to see you! Does this mean that spring is officially on the way?'

In reply, she pointed to the east, where the early morning sun was rising above the horizon, turning the wispy clouds above them the same shade of pink as her pretty blossoms.

'Hurray!' cheered Sycamore, bouncing up and down on a branch. Then he stopped. 'But what happened to the nasty winter weather? Did we

pay the
ransom?'
'Oh,
I don't
think so,'
Almond
Blossom said
gaily. 'There must
be something in the air,
I suppose . . .' She waved her flowery twig.
'Must dash! Don't forget about the Spring
Party!' She chuckled gleefully as she danced
away, leaving a stunned Sycamore behind
her.

Everything had turned out so well.
Understandably, the elves had been dubious
about her idea at first. They were utterly
dazzled by the promise of the six wonderful
sacks of magical fairy dust that awaited
them and were unwilling to give them up.

But, Almond Blossom made them feel so guilty with stories of the heartbroken Flower Fairies with tears dripping down their cheeks as they pined for spring that they gave in at last and agreed to lift the Winter

Cloud Spell. Because their stocks of elf dust were so low, Almond Blossom handed over the little silken bag – there were still a couple of handfuls of Windflower's precious fairy dust left – and made the elves promise to use it wisely before hitching a lift home with a friendly blackbird. Now, as she admired the glorious morning sky, Almond Blossom saw that the elves had kept their word.

'Joy! The winter's nearly gone!' she sang again, continuing her merry dance.

The Flower Fairies were so eager for the new season to arrive that the Spring Party was held the very next day. The garden was decked with as many pink flowers as Almond Blossom could spare and bunches of sunny yellow daffodils. Wildflower's tiny white flowers were scattered over the ground like fallen stars, while swathes of newly opened bluebells stretched as far as the eye could see. So much extra fairy dust had been made that week, it was sprinkled here and there. The glade gleamed and twinkled everywhere the Flower Fairies looked.

It was a wonderful party. Lots of familiar faces joined in the fun, but there were some unfamiliar faces too. Rush-Grass and Cotton-Grass had made the long journey

across the marsh – they turned out to be
excellent dancers – and three more visitors

weren't far behind.

The elves smiled sheepishly at Almond
Blossom as they sipped Elderberry's famous
juice from buttercups. 'Thank you for
inviting us,' mumbled the chief elf, fiddling
with his cuff.

'We love to dance,' said the second elf,
who was unable to stop his feet tapping.

'We just never get the chance,' said the third elf. 'Thank you.'

'It's the least I could do,' Almond Blossom replied. 'After all, you did return spring to us!'

And with that she winked at the elves and fluttered across to join her fairy friends at her favourite party of the year.

FLOWER
FAIRIES™
FRIENDS

Visit our Flower Fairies website at:

www.flowerfairies.com

There are lots of fun Flower Fairy games and
activities for you to play, plus you can find out more
about all your favourite fairy friends!

More tales from these Flower Fairies coming soon!

Strawberry

Candytuft

Sweet Pea